Winnie-the-Pooh and Some Bees

A.A. Milne

Illustrated by E.H. Shepard

METHUEN

Here is Edward Bear, coming downstairs now,

bump,

bump,

bump,

on the back of his head, behind Christopher Robin. It is, as far as he knows, the only way of coming downstairs,

but sometimes he feels that there really is another way, if only he could stop bumping for a moment and think of it. And then he feels that perhaps there isn't. Anyhow, here he is at the bottom, and ready to be introduced to you.

Winnie -the- Pooh.

When I first heard his name, I said, just as you are going to say, 'But I thought he was a boy?'

'So did I,' said Christopher Robin.

'Then you can't call him Winnie?'

'I don't.'

'But you said—'

'He's Winnie-ther-Pooh. Don't you know what "*ther*" means?'

'Ah, yes, now I do,' I said quickly; and I hope you do too, because it is all the explanation you are going to get.

Sometimes Winnie-the-Pooh likes a game of some sort when he comes downstairs, and sometimes he likes to sit quietly in front of the fire and listen to a story. This evening—

'What about a story?' said

Christopher Robin.

'*What* about a story?' I said.

'Could you very sweetly tell Winnie-the-Pooh one?'

'I suppose I could,' I said. 'What sort of stories does he like?'

'About himself. Because he's *that* sort of Bear.'

'Oh, I see.'

'So could you very sweetly?'

'I'll try,' I said.

So I tried.

Once upon a time,

a very long time ago now, about last Friday, Winnie-the-Pooh lived in a forest all by himself under the name of Sanders.

(*'What does "under the name" mean?'
asked Christopher Robin.*

'It means he had the name over the door in gold letters and lived under it.'

*'Winnie-the-Pooh wasn't quite sure,'
said Christopher Robin.*

'Now I am,' said a growly voice.

'Then I will go on,' said I.)

One day when he was out walking, he came to an open place in the middle of the forest, and in the middle of this place was a large oak-tree, and, from the top of the tree, there came a loud

buzzing-noise.

Winnie-the-Pooh
sat down at the foot
of the tree, put his head
between his paws, and began to think.
First of all he said to himself: 'That
buzzing-noise means
something. You don't get a
buzzing-noise like that,
just buzzing and buzzing,
without its meaning something.

'If there's a buzzing-noise, somebody's making a buzzing-noise, and the only reason for making a buzzing-noise that I know of is because you're a bee.'

Then he thought another long time, and said: 'And the only reason for being a bee that I know of is making honey.'

And then he got up, and said: 'And the only reason for making honey is so as *I* can eat it.' So he began to climb the tree. He climbed and he climbed and he climbed, and as he climbed he sang a little song to himself.

It went like this:

Isn't it funny ♪

♪ How a bear likes honey?

Buzz! Buzz! Buzz! ♪

I wonder why he does?

Then he climbed a little further . . . and a little further . . . and then just a little further. By that time he had thought of another song.

It's a very funny thought that, if Bears were Bees,

They'd build their nests at the bottom of trees.

And that being so (if the Bees were Bears),

We shouldn't have to climb up all these stairs.

He was getting rather tired by
this time, so that is why he sang a
Complaining Song. He was nearly
there now, and if he just stood on that
branch . . .

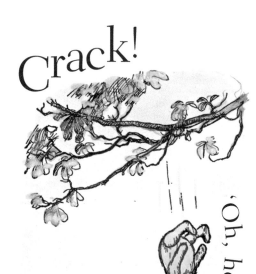

Crack!

'Oh, help!'

said Pooh, as he dropped ten feet
on to the branch below him.

'If only I hadn't—' he said,

as he bounced twenty feet on to the next branch.

'You see, what I *meant* to do,' he explained, as he turned head-over-heels, and crashed on to another branch thirty feet below, 'what I *meant* to do—'

'Of course, it *was* rather—' he admitted, as he slithered very quickly through the next six branches.

'It all comes, I suppose,' he decided, as he said good-bye to the last branch,

spun round three times, and flew
gracefully into a gorse-bush, 'it
all comes of *liking* honey so much.
Oh, *help!*'

He crawled out of the gorse-bush,

brushed the prickles from his nose, and began to think again. And the first person he thought of was Christopher Robin.

('Was that me?' said Christopher Robin in an awed voice, hardly daring to believe it.

'That was you.'

Christopher Robin said nothing, but his eyes got larger and larger, and his face got pinker and pinker.)

So Winnie-the-Pooh went round to his friend Christopher Robin, who

lived behind a green door in another
part of the Forest.

'Good morning, Christopher Robin,'
he said.

'Good morning, Winnie-*ther*-Pooh,'
said you.

'I wonder if you've got such a thing
as a balloon about you?'

'A balloon?'

'Yes, I just said to myself coming along:
"I wonder if Christopher Robin has such
a thing as a balloon about him?"

I just said it to myself, thinking of balloons, and wondering.'

'What do you want a balloon for?' you said.

Winnie-the-Pooh looked round to see that nobody was listening, put his paw to his mouth, and said in a deep whisper: '*Honey*!'

'But you don't get honey with balloons!'

'*I* do,' said Pooh.

Well, it just happened that you had been to a party the day before at the house of your friend Piglet, and you had balloons at the party.

You had had a big green balloon; and
one of Rabbit's relations had had a big
blue one, and had left it behind, being
really too young to go to a party at all;
and so you had brought the green one
and the blue one home with you.

'Which one would you like?' you asked
Pooh.

He put his head between his paws
and thought very carefully.

'It's like this,' he said. 'When you go
after honey with a balloon, the great

thing is not to let the bees know
you're coming. Now, if you have a
green balloon, they might think you
were only part of the tree, and not
notice you, and if you have a blue
balloon, they might think you were
only part of the sky, and not notice
you, and the question is: Which is
most likely?'

'Wouldn't they notice *you*
underneath the balloon?' you asked.

'They might or they might not,'

said Winnie-the-Pooh. 'You never
can tell with bees.' He thought for a
moment and said:

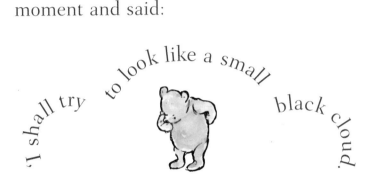

'I shall try to look like a small black cloud.

That will deceive them.'

'Then you had better have the blue
balloon,' you said; and so it was decided.

Well, you both went out with the blue balloon, and you took your gun with you, just in case, as you always did, and Winnie-the-Pooh went to a very muddy place that he knew of, and rolled and rolled . . .

until
he
was
black
all
over;

and then, when the
balloon was blown
up as big as big,
and you and Pooh
were both holding
on to the string,
you let go suddenly,
and Pooh Bear floated gracefully up into the sky . . .

and stayed there – level with the top
of the tree and about twenty feet away
from it.

'Hooray!' you shouted.

'Isn't that fine?' shouted Winnie-
the-Pooh down to you. 'What do I
look like?'

'You look like a Bear holding on to a
balloon,' you said.

'Not,' said Pooh anxiously, '—not like
a small black cloud in a blue sky?'

'Not very much.'

'Ah, well, perhaps from up here it looks different. And, as I say, you never can tell with bees.'

There was no wind to blow him nearer to the tree so there he stayed. He could see the honey, he could smell the honey, but he couldn't quite reach the honey.

After a little while he called down to you.

'Christopher Robin!' he said in a loud whisper.

'Hallo!'

'I think the bees *suspect* something!'

'What sort of thing?'

'I don't know. But something tells me that they're *suspicious*!'

'Perhaps they think that you're after their honey?'

'It may be that. You never can tell with bees.'

There was another little silence, and then he called down to you again.

'Christopher Robin!'

'Yes?'

'Have you an umbrella in your house?'

'I think so.'

'I wish you would bring it out here, and walk up and down with it, and look up at me every now and then, and say "Tut-tut, it looks like rain." I think, if you did that, it would help the deception which we are practising on these bees.'

Well, you laughed to yourself, 'Silly old Bear!' but you didn't say it aloud because you were so fond of him, and you went home for your umbrella.

'Oh, there you are!' called down
Winnie-the-Pooh, as soon as you got
back to the tree. 'I was beginning to get
anxious. I have discovered that the bees
are now definitely Suspicious.'

'Shall I put my umbrella up?' you said.

'Yes, but wait a moment. We must be
practical. The important bee to deceive
is the Queen Bee. Can you see which is
the Queen Bee from down there?'

'No.'

'A pity. Well, now, if you walk up
and down with your umbrella, saying,

"Tut-tut, it looks like rain,"

I shall do what I can by singing a little
Cloud Song, such as a cloud might
sing . . . Go!'

So, while you walked up and down and
wondered if it would rain, Winnie-the-
Pooh sang this song:

How sweet to be a Cloud ♪ Floating in the Blue!

Every little cloud ♪ Always sings aloud.

'How sweet to be a Cloud ♪

Floating in the Blue!' ♪

It makes him very proud ♪ To be a little cloud.

The bees were still buzzing as suspiciously as ever. Some of them, indeed, left their nests and flew all round the cloud as it began the second verse of this song, and one bee sat down on the nose of the cloud for a moment, and then got up again.

'Christopher – *OW!* – Robin,' called out the cloud.

'Yes?'

'I have just been thinking, and I have come to a very important decision.

These are the wrong sort of bees.'

'Are they?'

'Quite the wrong sort. So I should think they would make the wrong sort of honey, shouldn't you?'

'Would they?'

'Yes. So I think I shall come down.'

'How?' asked you.

Winnie-the-Pooh hadn't thought about this. If he let go of the string, he would fall . . . BUMP!

– and he didn't like the idea of that.
So he thought for a long time, and
then he said:

'Christopher Robin, you must shoot
the balloon with your gun. Have you got
your gun?'

'Of course I have,' you said. 'But if I do
that, it will spoil the balloon,' you said.

'But if you *don't*,' said Pooh, 'I shall
have to let go, and that would spoil *me*.'

When he put it like this, you saw how
it was, and you aimed very carefully at

the balloon, and fired.

'Ow!' said Pooh.

'Did I miss?' you asked.

'You didn't exactly *miss*,' said Pooh, 'but you missed the *balloon*.'

'I'm so sorry,' you said, and you fired again, and this time you hit the balloon, and the air came slowly out, and Winnie-the-Pooh floated down to the ground.

But his arms were so stiff from holding on to the string of the balloon

all that time that they stayed up
straight in the air for more than a
week, and whenever a fly came and
settled on his nose he had to blow
it off. And I think – but I am not

sure – that *that* is why he was always called Pooh.

*   *   *

'Is that the end of the story?' asked Christopher Robin.

'That's the end of that one. There are others.'

'About Pooh and Me?'

'And Piglet and Rabbit and all of you. Don't you remember?'

'I do remember, and then when I try

to remember, I forget.'

'That day when Pooh and Piglet tried to catch the Heffalump—'

'They didn't catch it, did they?'

'No.'

'Pooh couldn't, because he hasn't any brain. Did *I* catch it?'

'Well, that comes into the story.'

Christopher Robin nodded.

'I do remember,' he said, 'only Pooh doesn't very well, so that's why he likes having it told to him again.

Because then it's a real story and not just a remembering.'

'That's just how *I* feel,' I said.

Christopher Robin gave a deep sigh, picked his Bear up by the leg, and walked off to the door, trailing Pooh behind him. At the door he turned and said, 'Coming to see me have my bath?'

'I might,' I said.

'I didn't hurt him when I shot him, did I?'

'Not a bit.'

He nodded and went out, and in a
moment I heard Winnie-the-Pooh –
bump, bump, bump – going up the stairs
behind him.

Winnie-the-Pooh and Some Bees
is taken from *Winnie-the-Pooh*
originally published in
Great Britain 14 October 1926
by Methuen & Co. Ltd.
Text by A.A. Milne and line drawings by Ernest H. Shepard
copyright under the Berne Convention.

This edition published in Great Britain 2001
by Methuen Children's Books,
an imprint of Egmont Children's Books Limited,
a division of Egmont Holding Limited,
239 Kensington High Street, London W8 6SA.

1   3   5   7   9   10   8   6   4   2

Printed in China

ISBN 0 416 19955 0